R0061304747

10/2011

# Dog's New Coat

**by Margaret Nash**

## Illustrated by Lisa Williams

Crabtree Publishing Company

www.crabtreebooks.com

# Crabtree Publishing Company
**www.crabtreebooks.com**
1-800-387-7650

616 Welland Ave.
St. Catharines, ON
L2M 5V6

PMB 59051, 350 Fifth Ave.
59th Floor,
New York, NY

Published by Crabtree Publishing in 2011

**Series Editor:** Jackie Hamley
**Editor:** Reagan Miller
**Series Advisor:** Catherine Glavina
**Series Designer:** Peter Scoulding
**Project Coordintor:** Kathy Middleton

Text © Margaret Nash 2010
Illustration © Lisa Williams 2010

Printed in Hong Kong/042011/BK20110304

First published in 2010
by Franklin Watts
(A division of Hachette
Children's Books)

The rights of the author and the
illustrator of this Work have
been asserted.

**Library and Archives Canada
Cataloguing in Publication**

Nash, Margaret, 1939-
    Dog's new coat / by Margaret Nash ; illustrated by
Lisa Williams.

(Tadpoles)
ISBN 978-0-7787-0576-5 (bound).--
ISBN 978-0-7787-0587-1 (pbk.)

    I. Williams, Lisa, 1970- II. Title.
III. Series: Tadpoles (St. Catharines, Ont.)

PZ10.3.N175Do 2011        j823'.914        C2011-900151-9

**Library of Congress
Cataloging-in-Publication Data**

Nash, Margaret, 1939-
 Dog's new coat / by Margaret Nash ; illustrated by
Lisa Williams.
    p. cm. -- (Tadpoles)
    Summary: When Dog gets a new spotted coat he
quickly decides he does not like it, but every time he
tries to get rid of the coat it comes back to him.
  ISBN 978-0-7787-0587-1 (pbk. : alk. paper) --
ISBN 978-0-7787-0576-5 (reinforced library binding :
alk. paper)
 [1. Dogs--Fiction. 2. Individuality--Fiction. 3. Contentment
--Fiction.] I. Williams, Lisa, 1970- ill. II. Title. III. Series.

PZ7.N1732Dog 2011
[E]--dc22
                                        2010052361

Here is a list of the words in this story.
Common words:

| | | |
|---|---|---|
| a | got | the |
| at | his | to |
| back | in | too |
| but | it | was |
| came | now | went |

Other words:

| | | | |
|---|---|---|---|
| car | left | park | spotty |
| coat | likes | school | store |
| dog | new | | |

# Dog got a new coat.

# But it was too spotty.

5

# Dog left it in the store.

But the coat
came back.

9

# Dog left it in the car.

But the coat
came back.

# Dog left it at school.

14

But the coat
came back.

17

# Dog went to the park.

# Dog likes his spotty coat now!

21

# Puzzle Time

a

b

Can you find these pictures in the story?

**c**

**d**

Which pages are
the pictures from?

**Turn over for the answers!**

## Answers

The pictures come from these pages:
a. pages **6** and **7**
b. pages **18** and **19**
c. pages **12** and **13**
d. pages **20** and **21**

# Notes for adults

**Tadpoles** are structured to provide support for early readers. The stories may also be used by adults for sharing with young children.

Starting to read alone can be daunting. **Tadpoles** help by listing the words in the book for a preview before reading. **Tadpoles** also provide strong visual support and repeat words and phrases. These books will both develop confidence and encourage reading and rereading for pleasure.

**If you are reading this book with a child, here are a few suggestions:**

1. Make reading fun! Choose a time to read when you and the child are relaxed and have time to share the story.

2. Look at the picture on the front cover and read the blurb on the back cover. What might the story be about? Why might the child like it?

3. Look at the list of words on page two. Can the child identify most of the words?

4. Encourage the child to retell the story using the jumbled picture puzzle on pages 22-23.

5. Discuss the story and see if the child can relate it to his or her own experiences, or perhaps compare it to another story he or she knows.

6. Give praise! Children learn best in a positive environment.

If you enjoyed this book, why not try another **TADPOLES** story?
Please see the back cover for more **TADPOLES** titles.
Visit **www.crabtreebooks.com** for other **Crabtree** books.